KARI NICHOLS

A Dysfunctional Life

Edited by Melissa Harlow
Proofread by Traci Craft - www.craftreads.com
Cover design by Kari Nichols

Author photograph by Cottonwood Studios
            (http://www.cottonwoodstudiosworldwide.com)
Title font: Impact Label by Michael Tension
            (http://www.twitter.com/mtension)
Handwriting font: Good Foot by Jakob Fischer
            (http://www.pizzadude.dk)

For more information about Kari Nichols, please visit:

www.KariNichols.com

For my mother.

Your unfailing positivity and faith will never cease to amaze me. You were born with a purpose.

You are loved.

COMMITTED

I HEAD HOME from school with my backpack on my back. My long blond ponytail and peach sundress are disheveled from the long day of listening to boring lectures and taking tests. Most Thursday afternoons I walk the ten blocks home from school, but today the heat of the fast-approaching summer got the best of me. The bus is full of noisy middle-schoolers, but my street is the first stop on the bus route, so I don't mind the deafening squeals.

I get off the bus and walk through our lawn. It's hot today —usually my mother waters the lawn when it's this hot, but the dry grass crunches under my feet. I step through the front door of our comfortable middle-class home, where I'm usually greeted by an excited mother and dog, along with an aloof cat that generally pretends I'm another plant blending in with the scenery. Today, there's no one.

"Hello? Anyone here?" I ask, confused by the absence of my welcoming committee.

No response.

I take off my backpack and head to the kitchen, where I

know an after-school snack will be awaiting my homecoming. No snack is sitting in its normal place on the kitchen counter. I look around, feeling stumped. What in the world could have happened to create this break in our long-standing tradition?

No welcoming committee. No snack.

I look up from the counter and spot her. My mother is hunched over in a kitchen chair, looking despondent.

"Mom? Are you okay? What's going on?" I ask tentatively, without receiving a response. 'Catatonic mother' is never a good sign. And it's not a side of my mother I've seen before. I can feel my level of panic rising as my mind starts to scream that something is horribly wrong with this picture. Next to my mother's chair there's a black trash bag on the floor—the kind we always use for the raked leaves and yard clippings in the spring and fall.

"What's in the bag?" I ask, confused about why a trash bag might be sitting on our kitchen floor.

My mother finally turns and looks up at me. I gasp as I take in her defeated expression and beaten face. I walk slowly toward her while I systematically catalog what my eyes are seeing. Her green eyes are red and puffy from crying. Her right eye is heavily bruised—something or someone gave her a black eye. There's a long scratch down her right cheek that bled earlier, but the blood has since dried, and the scratch has started to scab over. A dark bruise looks like it's wrapping its way up her right arm, and the knuckles and fingers on her left hand are bloody and bruised.

I stare at her, unmoving, in shock. My brain is incapable of forming coherent thoughts. I make a sound somewhere between a questioning grunt and a cry, which seems to snap my mother out of her silence.

"I had to commit your brother today. He came home from school early and started screaming about how I force him to go to school against his will. I told him I didn't know what he was talking about. He's never disliked school in the past, and he's a senior! Did you see that he was having problems?" she asks, her mind still foggy from the day's events.

My feet are nailed to the ground. *What did she say? My brother's been committed? As in, a psychiatric ward?* I can't wrap my head around what she's saying to me. Surely this is some sick joke or misunderstanding.

"What are you talking about, mom?" I ask in a hushed whisper.

"He attacked me," my mother says as she begins to weep so hard she's hyperventilating.

I run to her to hold her, but she pulls back as I approach. She's scared of me. I suppose after what she's been through, she has a right to be scared. The bruises on her face and arm will only look worse tomorrow. I sit in the chair next to her, take her hand softly in mine, and give it a small, reassuring squeeze.

"He just came after me. I've never seen anything like it. I was screaming, and he was yelling. It was chaos. I got him off of me, and he ran to his room, still yelling about how terrible his life is. I called the police, and they took him to St. Vincent's psych ward to be committed for treatment. The doctors are running tests and doing brain scans. No one has any idea what's going on."

I can't move. I can barely breathe. I can't comprehend what she's talking about. My brother? My brother?

"He killed them. After he went to his room, I found them both dead," she sobs, as she looks down at the black trash bag on the floor.

My heart sinks at her words.

"What's in the bag, mom? Tell me right now—what's in the bag?" I demand.

I already know the answer. My cat and dog are in the bag. They're dead.

"He killed the animals," she whimpers, barely loud enough for me to hear.

I stand up—carefully and without any sudden movements —and walk slowly to the home phone. I grab it and tiptoe up the stairs to my small room. This scenario has been haunting me for years. I only ever wanted a stable home with a kind mother or father, and I got to live out that fantasy in this house for years. But I realize with despondency that my desperate prayers for a continued life of happiness have gone unanswered, and my worst fear has finally been realized. I close and lock the door and sit down on the edge of my bed. I force my breathing to slow as I stare down at the phone and dial 911.

"911. What's your emergency?" the voice answers.

"I need you to come to my house and pick up my mother," I say as quietly as I can manage.

"Okay. Can you tell me what's wrong with her?" the voice asks calmly.

My head starts spinning. *How can I explain this?* There's only one thought repeating in my head. Over and over. Only one thought. I let out a single, choked sob before speaking.

"I'm an only child."

NAMELESS

AS I SIT in my office, I glance out my second-story window at the homeless man across the street. He always sits in the same place on the sidewalk. His gray disheveled hair and wrinkled suntanned skin look the same as usual. And the dirty dress shirt and faded slacks (I can't tell if they've always been gray or if they started out black at some point) with rips in the knees and hem are situated the exact same way as they have been every day since he showed up on this block.

He always talks—to whom, no one knows. Some days, people sit with him and listen or ask him questions. I gave it a go a few times, but I couldn't get anywhere with him. He wouldn't tell me his name or where he was from or anything truly personal. I thought maybe if I could get some information on him, I could search for him in a missing person's database, but he was always vague with his response. No matter what I asked, he always repeated the exact same story with little or no deviation. So I gave up. Still, on slow days like today, I sometimes watch him from my office window.

He always starts the same way:

I've lived on the streets since I was 41.

I try not to keep track of time so much now. It only reminds me of days past.

Don't look at me like that. I know you're thinking I sound too educated to be living on the streets. But don't judge me.

How did I end up here? Well, that's the magic question, isn't it? Anyone who talks to me anymore either asks me if I need a place to go, or if I need a dollar, or how I ended up out here on my own. When people ask that question, I pull a 'crazy' and start screaming or mumbling so they'll leave me alone. I don't like to share with strangers. There's nothing they need to know about me, and there's nothing I need to know about them. Unless they're giving me a crossword puzzle—in which case I'll sit and listen to their whole life story.

But I guess I'll go ahead and get this out of the way since I can tell you're not gonna let it go. A few years back, I lost my whole family in a week. I'm not going to elaborate on that one, but just know they're gone. Really gone. And there's nothing I can do to get them back. I was a successful businessman before everything imploded. My family was happily middle class, and we lived in a nice neighborhood. I wore a suit every day. I was clean-shaven! Can you even imagine that? I can't any more.

But once I got out here, I found friends—real friends. Friends who didn't care what kind of car I drove, or if I had a beautiful home, or if my wife was pretty. They just took me as I was and showed me the ropes.

When everything first fell apart, I just left. I dropped everything and walked out. I didn't even know where I was going. I started walking, and I didn't stop until I got here. The only thing I had, apart from the clothes I was wearing, was a crossword puzzle folded up in my pocket. My buddies over there could tell something was troubling me, so they took me in, fed me, and gave me a place to sleep. I was so overjoyed at the prospect of a new life, I didn't care that my bed was a dirty sheet in a cardboard box. I still don't care. I'm just blessed to be here, with people who care about me. My old life was surrounded by people who, I found out the hard way, had never cared about me. But that's why I'm here.

Now I just sit here with my cup for donations and my sign next to me. I don't use the money for drugs and alcohol. My buddies over there think I'm weird, but I only have room in my life for one vice. It's the one thing I brought with me from my old life. Most of my days are filled with crossword puzzles. I never could pass up a good crossword.

Hey, do you have a crossword puzzle I could have? Or a few bucks to spare? I could really use a bite to eat.

He blinks a few times and looks around, realizing he's talking to no one. There's nothing but thin air around him.

I shake my head and turn back to my desk. The second he's out of my sight, my mind turns back to my paperwork. And just like that, the nameless man is forgotten once again.

THE ARGUMENT

"HOW MANY TIMES do we need to have this argument?" I ask, annoyed by the endless cycle we seem to be stuck in.

We may have made it through six years of marriage, but we still haven't figured out how to do it well. I'm a neurotic control freak with too many addictions to count on my appendages. My husband is so lazy, and disinterested in life itself, that he doesn't give two shits about all my issues. He adopted a go-with-the-flow mentality at a young age. You see, his mother was just like me—a neurotic, alcoholic sex-addict with almost as many issues as I have. She died from an overdose when Chip was in elementary school. That's my husband's name—Chip ... or at least that's what everyone calls him. His real name was Chelsea—his mother really wanted a daughter and decided to take her anger out on Chip for entering the world with a penis. But he doesn't care. He happily adopted the nickname his dad gave him as a child and ended up legally changing his name to Chip during college. But that's neither here nor there.

The argument. We've probably had this same argument over a hundred times in the past six years. It's the one point of tension I found that Chip will actually get worked up about.

He doesn't get upset when he catches me using. He could care less whether or not I drink myself into a stupor night after night. He only got slightly irritated when he found out I cheated on him. But this—this is his hot button. I always know I can get a rise out of him if I bring it up.

And maybe that's the point. Maybe my neurotic, addictive personality needs him to care about *something*. I probably bring it up time and time again just so he'll react.

I've grown so tired of his indifference over the years, that maybe I just need the attention. As I realize the probability of that being my intention, tears gather in the corners of my eyes.

He's never fought for me. Not once. When he discovered my drug abuse, he shrugged and told me I should probably stop—as if it was an inevitability that I would use again and again, and nothing he said could stop me.

When I started getting drunk every night, he just rolled his eyes and turned his attention fully to the television. He's never tried to take away the alcohol. He's never told me to stop acting like a child.

When I cheated on him the first time, I *wanted* to get caught. I intentionally invited the faceless nobody over to sleep with me in *our* bed. And when Chip walked in, he had the audacity to apologize *to me*! I screamed in frustration and kicked the adulterous man—yes, he was married too—out of the house. Every time I've cheated on Chip since then, he just shrugs and says "okay." As if he simply has to accept it and move on.

But every horrible thing I've done over the past six years was for Chip. I know that makes me sound insane. And I'm not going to deny it. I already told you I have more issues than anyone would know what to do with.

Here's my problem:

After we got married, Chip stopped trying to impress me. He stopped taking me out on dates. He stopped trying to hold my hand in public. He stopped flirting. He just ... quit.

So I felt it was my responsibility to try. I did anything and everything I could think of to force him to make an effort. But nothing worked. And after a few years, I gave up. Well, I never really gave up, but I stopped hoping. The only evidence that I still haven't given up is the argument. I need to have the argument at least once a month so I know he still—in some small way—cares enough to stay.

"Why will you not just divorce me and get it over with?" I scream at the top of my lungs.

"Why would I do that? I love you! I don't care what you do

to try to get me to leave. If you want a divorce, you're going to have to be the one to walk away," he says with as much passion as he has in every previous argument on the topic over the past six years.

And that's it. I need to hear it at least once a month just to know for sure.

"Fine!" I scream.

As I turn around and walk away, I smile and heave a sigh of relief.

He still loves me. That's all I needed to hear.

THE SECRET

I'VE BEEN KEEPING a secret for far too long. A secret that isn't mine to tell. Unfortunately, the person the secret belongs to is no longer a part of my life, but I'm haunted every day by the burden I've carried for so long.

He was my best friend from the first time we met. We were six years old, walking into our very first day of school. We looked at each other and exchanged tentative smiles. That was all it took for me.

"Hi! It's nice to meet you!" I said as I thrust my hand out toward him. When he shook my hand, he looked at me like I was terrifying and amazing at the same time.

I was the outgoing one. He was the shy one.

As we grew up, I helped him come out of his shell. We played basketball together starting in third grade, and it quickly became evident that he was going to be the best on the team. He worked harder than everyone else AND had more natural talent. The only reason I was good enough to be on the team was because if I wanted to spend any quality time with him outside of school, I had to practice with him. It didn't bother me at all, though. My dad was thrilled that my best friend was helping me strive toward excellence. In life, I've almost always taken the path of least resistance. But because of him, I became a pretty good ball player.

He told me he was keeping a secret when we were twelve years old. I bugged, prodded, and begged him to tell me the secret for two months before he finally broke down.

"You swear you'll never tell a soul?" he asked, still unsure if he should confide in me.

"I will take it to my grave. I won't tell anyone. Not ever. Not even if I'm being tortured by Nazis," I swore faithfully (we had just studied World War II in history class).

I still remember his horrified expression as he revealed his secret to me. Of course, I thought nothing of it. I told him the secret was safe forever, and we went back to shooting hoops. Nothing could or would ever come between us.

Or so I thought.

I always believed if something were to separate us, it would be a big argument over a girl or some major life decision. I never could've dreamed that the stupid secret would be the nail in the coffin of our friendship.

I've kept my promise all these years. I miss my best friend horribly—I haven't talked to him for what feels like an eternity. I often find myself wishing I could just call him up and chat.

And I always stop myself right before I pick up the phone.

But no matter what, just like I promised, I'll keep his secret 'til the day I die.

FIVE MORE

"ONLY FIVE MORE to go," I say quietly.

My workout started out slow. I've never been one for sports or athletic activity. I chose an easier—or more difficult, depending on how you see it—route for staying thin. But after a terrifying trip to the hospital, I was forced to make a change.

Before, I would drink a glass of orange juice and let it sit in my stomach for a few minutes to enjoy the feeling of having something, anything, in my stomach. Then I would take a trip to the bathroom to evacuate it. One can never be too careful with weight. Even a glass of orange juice could potentially add half a pound to a body.

Now I have an egg each morning for breakfast with a cup of coffee. I sit and eat slowly, enjoying every bite. I make myself have a few carrot sticks between breakfast and lunch. Then I eat a tuna fish sandwich for lunch. Once I hit 3 pm, I eat half an apple. And every night for dinner I have two small pieces of chicken and some sort of vegetable. My doctor still isn't satisfied with how much I'm eating, but at least she knows I'm not throwing up after every bite.

I wasn't always this way. I grew up thinking I was one of the beautiful people. Hell, I was a member of the popular group at school, from kindergarten all the way through high school. I was on homecoming court every year, and I was even homecoming queen my senior year. But. My junior year of high school I started dating the coolest guy in school. I had basically been in love with him since middle school. No matter what I did, he always looked repulsed by me. If we were kissing, he could hardly stand to touch me for longer than a few seconds. There were no make-out sessions. No fooling around. Definitely no sex. I tried everything. But he didn't seem to be interested in breaking up with me, and I was madly in love with him. I knew if I didn't change something, I might lose him. So I decided something had to be done.

I took matters into my own hands.

I remember asking him what was wrong with me. He told me it was him, not me. As if that line hadn't been used a trillion times.

I lost a few pounds. I tried to get him to look at me as if I weren't the most repulsive thing he had ever seen. No luck.

I lost some more weight. My parents started worrying about me and took me to the doctor. But I swore up and down I was fine. No one was convinced. Even my boyfriend started worrying about me. He took extra care to get us both food in the cafeteria, and of course I always ate what he brought me. But a few minutes later, I would throw it up. I don't mean to make him out to be a heartless bastard. The guy was one of the most genuinely caring, loving people I've ever known. It's why I fell in love with him in the first place. It's why I always knew that I was the issue. I was the only one that was dating him, and I was the only one he looked at with distaste. He never wanted to touch me sexually, so I didn't force the issue.

Six months later, the night before graduation, he killed himself. We were still together. Still virgins. And I knew I had driven him to his death. His family life was happy. His friends all loved him. I was making him unhappy. And I've never forgiven myself.

For five years after his death, I continued my eating habits. I would sit and wonder if I was insane, but I always ended the conversation with, "At least you're not a psychopath like your sister—a drug-addicted, alcoholic sex fiend with a husband who couldn't care less." I always felt better after repeating that line. Because the only person who I was hurting in my quest to stay thin was me.

Then, one day, I ended up in a hospital, IVs in my arm. And I decided I needed to make a change. So I hired a nutritionist, a therapist, and an athletic trainer. I fought all of them for the first year, but eventually I caved to their wishes. I still weigh twenty pounds less than a woman my size should weigh (according to my nutritionist), but I haven't revisited the hospital since that awful day.

The ten year anniversary of my boyfriend's death is this week. And I think I'm going to survive it.

I refocus my mind on the free weights I hold in my hands. *Only five more to go.*

A LIFE OF PURPOSE

I BELIEVE that every life has a purpose. I've seen too many happy coincidences to believe otherwise.

After seventy-four years on this earth, that's the only thing I can be sure of.

My son disappeared after his baby passed away. Just up and left without so much as a "love you, mom." But his life had a purpose. I know my son has brought me years of suffering by not telling me where he went, but in the lifetime he lived before that, he was an angel.

He was always a respectful man—even from a young age. And that won him the esteem of everyone who met him. He was a good student, a great husband, and an excellent son. His boss and co-workers all loved him. But after my grandbaby died, he just disappeared.

The police stopped searching for him six months after his disappearance, and his wife decided he was dead. But a mother knows, and my son is still alive. He's still out there. And my dream is that he's touching people's lives the way he did when he was growing up.

See, I'm no stranger to loss. My mother and father died when I was a child. I was the youngest of five siblings. They all passed away over the years—two from cancer, one from a heart attack—and until last year, it was just my oldest brother and me that were left. But he was ten years older than I, and he passed away from old age.

My husband and I had twenty-five years of joy together before he was killed in a car accident. We were hit head-on by a drunk driver. Our three kids were in the back seat, and as soon as he figured out that we were going to get hit, my husband angled the car so the front left corner would receive the full impact of the crash. He was the only one who died.

Four years later, my youngest boy was diagnosed with bone cancer—a rarity for an eighteen-year-old, but he only lasted a year before passing away. Two years after that, my only daughter was on a climbing expedition with her husband when part of the mountain broke away, and they both fell to their deaths. So when I say, "I'm no stranger to loss," I mean it.

I know for sure that my oldest boy is still alive. It felt different when he left. The gaping hole that's left in a mother's heart when her child passes away wasn't there. And if he was dead, it would be. He was always my favorite. Still is. He's just my favorite in another life.

I don't know why I've outlived almost everyone I know and

love. There isn't any explanation for it. But I keep my joy. I pray every day—especially for my boy. And people are always telling me I'm an inspiration to them to continue to live with joy no matter what happens in life.

I'm not sure what other choice I have. But I do know I have a purpose. Everyone does.

HAPPY BIRTHDAY

WHEN I WAS fifteen years old, my boyfriend and I got pregnant. We hadn't meant to be so stupid about our sexual activity, but we were both too afraid to buy condoms.

As soon as we read the test, my heart sank. I knew for sure I was going to have to tell my parents ... and they thought I was a virgin. I still remember the conversation.

"I have to tell you guys something, and I need you to promise me you won't flip out on me," I said, determined to stay strong. I could feel the cracks of my carefully-placed, determined exterior crumbling like a dilapidated wall under the weight of a too-heavy roof.

"What's going on, Honey? You're worrying us," my mother said lovingly.

My parents were excessively conservative. I didn't know what kind of reaction to expect. But I assumed it would either border on maniacal anger or depressed denial.

"I messed up. I took a test last night, and I'm pregnant." I distinctly remember finishing that sentence as more of a question than a statement. I waited as my parents' faces grew contorted with emotion. Shock, pain, confusion, anger, grief, determination. Those were the expressions I could pinpoint in my parents' faces over the sixty seconds of silence following my delivery of the news. My mother and father exchanged a look I'd never seen before. Then she looked at me and spoke.

"If you're old enough to have sex, then you're old enough to carry a child. We can decide together whether or not you want to raise the baby or put it up for adoption over the next several months. But you *will* have that baby. And you *will* go to school. This is going to feel like an impossible task. But you got yourself into this mess with a bad decision. And I won't let you get yourself out of it by making a worse one."

I don't think a day has gone by since that moment that I haven't thought of her words. They changed my life. Initially, I was mortified at the idea of having to go to school pregnant. But then I realized I never would have been able to abort the baby anyway. So what other option was there?

When I delivered my daughter fifteen years ago, I kissed her cheeks and told her she was beautiful. And before I said my tearful goodbye, I whispered softly in her tiny ear, "Happy birthday, my little girl. Mommy loves you."

I knew the family that would take her in would be much better suited to raise a child. But this day every year—her birthday—I wish I could have known her. I wonder what she's like, if she looks like me or her dad, if she's making all the same bad decisions I made at her age, or if she's a better person than I was. I pray she's smarter than me. And I hope she has parents that will respond as well as mine did when I told them I was having a baby. I pray for her to be happy.

I have my own family now—a husband and two kids. I've never told them about my first baby. But they know every year, on this day, I go out by myself. And every year, I come home with a red face and puffy eyes.

Happy fifteenth birthday, my little girl. Mommy still loves you.

CHANGING HISTORY

I'VE BEEN reliving that day in my head at least once a week since it happened. And for the past few months, I've relived it more frequently. I used to remember it exactly as it happened—with no deviation from the truth. But this month has been different. Every time I remember it, I somehow change my reaction or response time. I alter reality so that, instead of the tragic outcome that I've lived with all these years, the ending of the story is transformed—still sad, but easier for me to cope with. A shift has begun to take shape in my mental soundness. I've started believing the other version of what happened. And even though I understand the mental breakdown that comes with every delusion, I'm so desperate for a different ending that I'm willing to sacrifice my sanity. I know what's coming next, and I don't care.

I pull out the letter every year and read it. Somehow, I know this will be the last time.

Dear Mom and Dad,

I'm so sorry. I'm sorry for what I know you must be going through. You didn't even know I was unhappy.

Mom, I'm so sorry I pushed you away today. I've reached my breaking point, but I never meant to hurt you or yell at you. I really hope you don't have any bruises. I couldn't have asked for a more perfect mom. Coming home from school every afternoon to be greeted by you, an afternoon snack, and our dog has been one of my favorite parts of every day.

Dad, you're the best dad in the world. You've shown me the kind of man that I always wanted to be kind, fair, strong, loving, and you provide for your family. Thank you for always pushing me to be the best at whatever I tried my hand at.

You two have done nothing you should regret. My life has been amazing. But for me, it's been a lie.

I'm gay. I always have been. And I know you wouldn't have turned me away because of it, but I also know you would never have approved. This way is easier. You don't have to tell your friends. You don't have to tell the family. I just needed the two of you to know why I'm gone. I couldn't take the pressure of coming out to everyone. No one would have understood or believed. And I would have been mocked, ridiculed, rejected or preached at by everyone in my life.

Don't tell people. I don't want people to blame the two of you for my turning out this way or for my decision to end my life ... and I know that's how people would respond ... because people suck.

But I need you to tell a few people some final words for me.

Tell Chip he's my best friend. Tell him thank you for being the one person I trusted with my secret. Tell him thank you for keeping it for all these years and for not letting it change the way he saw me. Tell him he better keep playing basketball or else. And tell him I owe him forever ... even in the afterlife.

Tell Bekah she was an amazing girlfriend. It was never her ... it was always me. She's gorgeous no matter what she eats ... no matter how little or how much she weighs.

Tell grandma I'm gonna miss her. It was her positivity that kept me going for so long. And tell her I love her.

I'm so sorry. I know this might be selfish of me ... the easy way out. But I've thought about it long and hard, and I just don't want to shame you two at church. I can't take the ridicule that I know would be waiting for me at school. And I don't have the energy to pretend I'm a happy, girl-crazy, heterosexual guy any more.

I love you both. Thank you for raising me in such a happy home.

-Evan

No matter how many years go by, the letter never gets easier to read. When we found him, we tried everything to revive him. But he had taken so many pills, there was no bringing him back. After we read the letter, we sat at the kitchen table for hours. My husband walked out the door, still dressed from work that day, and I never saw him again. The police quit looking for him six months later. But from the look he had on his face when he walked out, I wouldn't be surprised if he took his own life. After the police gave up, I had to face the fact that he was never coming home again. I began to live as if he was dead—and that's what I told all our friends and family. My husband's mental breakdown was immediate. Mine has taken ten years.

I heard a few years ago that Bekah finally got medical help for her eating disorder. Poor girl always thought Evan hadn't liked her because she was too fat. But he simply hadn't liked girls that way. I honored his wishes and never told anyone.

I went to counseling for a few years before I decided I wanted to adopt a kid to fill the Evan-sized hole in my heart. After a long case study on the suitability of my home and mental status, I got a precious daughter who was eight years old. Poor thing had lost her last set of parents to a car accident. What she didn't know was that they had adopted her as a newborn baby. I was given her full history when I got her seven years ago, but she was never told that she had been adopted as an infant, so I let her believe the lie her last parents fed her. No harm in never knowing you were unwanted, right? My only regret with trying to relive the past and changing the way things happen is that, in my alternate reality, I never get to adopt my little girl. Maybe I'll add her in this time. I could've adopted her and still had Evan.

I smile as that afternoon begins again in my head. This time, when Evan comes home and screams for me to get out of his way, I really fight back. He gets so angry that he leaves bruises on my arms and even scratches my face on accident. He goes so crazy, he kills both the cat and the dog. When he runs to his room, I immediately call 911. When they show up, they stop him from taking the pills in his room, and he's taken to the psych ward at St. Vincent's for treatment. Once I've filled out all the paperwork and the nurses check my wounds, I return home to clean up the cat and dog. I don't want my husband and daughter to have to see them bloodied on the floor when they get home. I put both animals in a trash bag that I'll bury in the backyard later, and I clean up all the blood.

When I'm finished, I sit down at the kitchen table and try to figure out how to explain the day's events to my family.

For the first time, I don't rouse from the fantasy. I don't regret a single action. This is how I should always have responded. And here I sit ... changing history.

ACKNOWLEDGEMENTS

FIRST and foremost, I'd like to thank my Lord and Savior for giving me a life beyond my wildest dreams. It's because of Him that I'm able to live in the best city in the U.S. and spend my days writing.

Thanks to my husband for his unending support and love.

I would also like to thank Melissa, my editor, and Traci, my proofreader, for once again making my work a thousand times better than it originally was. Your feedback is invaluable to me. It means so much that I have people I love and trust as a part of my process.

Lastly, I'd once again like to thank the people who buy and read my work. I appreciate you so much. Just knowing that my stories are finding good homes would be enough, but the fact that you encourage and support me on social media and in face-to-face interactions is mind-blowing. I hope I can continue to live up to your expectations. I love you all.

One final thought about this collection of stories: lives matter. **All** lives matter. Never rejoice in a life lost. Never judge a person simply by what you hear or see about them. There is so much more to a person than what happens in view of the public eye. Everyone has a story and a past. The important thing in life is to **love**. Love others as you love yourself. And always remember—all lives matter.

KARI NICHOLS

was inspired to write after moving from Arkansas to the colorful and energetic city of New York. Her passion for creating art was developed from the time she was a child. Her artistic endeavors have ranged from music composition to photography to fashion design, but writing novels is far and away her favorite artistic outlet. She can often be found wrapped up in her favorite blanket, writing her next novel with a cup of hot tea in hand. She is a self-professed nerd, and when she isn't writing, she loves to play video games, read romance novels, and go on international adventures with her charming husband.

You can visit her online at

WWW.KARINICHOLS.COM

or on Twitter (@TheKariNichols)

www.ingramcontent.com/pod-product-compliance
Lightning Source LLC
Chambersburg PA
CBHW020606130626
46552CB00007B/3064